Campfire Stories for kids

a Collection of Short Spooky and Mystery Tales -
Scary Ghost Legends to Tell for Children in the Dark

Nicole Goodman

Table of contents

The Nun Who Loves to Help 4

Forgotten by The Campfire 12

The Birthday Clown 19

The Haunted Snowman 27

The Girl in The Hotel 35

Billie Lost His Boo! 43

Stay Away from The Thirteenth Floor 51

The Eleventh Ghost.. 60

The One Who Cried Tory 67

The Candy Woman 72

The Uninvited Guest 81

A Chilly Night 92

Mirror, Mirror on The Wall 99

YOUR FREE GIFT

As a way of saying thanks for your purchase, we're offering the book "Knock Knock Jokes for Kids" (regularly priced at $9.99 on Amazon) for FREE to our readers. In this book, you'll find over 500 fantastic jokes for hours of fun for the whole family.

In addition, you'll also have an opportunity to get our new books for FREE!

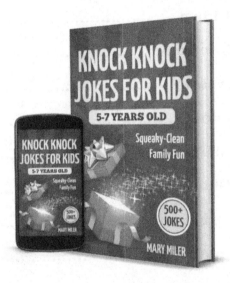

To get your Free Gift go to link: bit.ly/43WKetK

or scan QR code with your camera

The Nun Who Loves to Help

In an old folks home was a nun who knew nothing other than to take care of elderly people. All her life, she wanted nothing more than to give the old folks the happiness they deserved during their aging years.

While everyone around her knew of her passion, no one knew *how* she had come to devote her life to treating the elderly. Some say she was raised by her grandparents, resulting in treating her elders with so much love and compassion, while others believe she was just a person with a heart of gold.

She used to take care of a lot of elderly folks, tending to their every need. She adored each one as if they shared the same blood. And when they would close their eyes for all eternity, she would bawl with great sadness, realizing how little time she had had with them.

She hated to see her patients go, but she was especially protective of one man. Mr. Davis had a special place in the nun's heart because he treated her like his own child. At the ripe old age of seventy-one, the old man still had some muscle in his slowing body. However, his legs were getting more frail with his knees aching as if he had run a marathon every day. His back was cracking with every few steps take, leaving him unable to move any further than the front gate of the old folk's home.

The nun was happy to care for this old man who seemed to have been abandoned by those who were supposed to love him.

"How cruel of them!" she thought with rage. Mr. Davis had two sons who had left him in this place one day when their father wasn't able to move on his own. But she also felt thankful toward his sons because she got to meet the old man and take care of him.

If she couldn't make these old folk happy, no one could!

One day, the nun was getting ready to help Mr. Davis with some activities. She was walking inside the room she shared with another nurse to fetch something when she spotted the latter packing her belongings in a suitcase.

"Where are you going? To see your family?" the nun asked with curiosity.

The nurse shook her head and replied, "No, I have been fired."

The nun gasped in horror. What about the patient she was looking after? Who will the old person be handed to? The caring nun expected to take her place; she knew that no one would look after the old folks the way she did.

"But why?" the nun asked, her face was covered in disbelief.

The other nurse then told her everything, and what she heard broke her heart. Not for a good reason, however. The nurse was packing up to leave... for good. She had been laid off! The old-folks home was losing money, so they had to fire some of the staff. Plus, the nurse's patient had gotten healthy enough to contact his family to take him back.

The nun seethed with more rage but was also overcome with fear. Fear that like the nurse and the others who had gone, she too would get fired and lose her patient, Mr. Davis. If they were willing to kick their own staff out, then she might be next! If Mr. Davis started getting well and was sent back home, she would have no one left to look after.

She would have to leave the very place that made her feel so alive! The nun would not stand for it. She wanted to stay but, more importantly, she wanted Mr. Davis to stay! Only if he stayed could the nun stay too.

But much to her dismay, as time went by, the nun had begun to hear everyone saying how much Mr. Davis was fully recovering. The nun, being the loving woman she was, smiled, looking as if she was witnessing a miracle. In truth, there was nothing in her but pure fear.

Mr. Davis was becoming healthier...

She was busy taking care of new patients which made her unable to take the time to go and witness the miracle with her own eyes. However, she wished it wasn't true.

That same night, the nun could not get a wink of sleep. She was out of her room getting some water when she saw Mr. Davis standing above the stairs. It was the first time since the rumors that she had seen him. Mr. Davis was on his way to get some fresh air while climbing down the stairs, and that image was like a nightmare to her. His legs did not wobble or crack, and his back was regaining its posture. He still had his cane, but he didn't even attempt to call for the nun to help him down like he used to just a few weeks back.

The nun's eyes widened and her heart was pounding. They had not been lying. Mr. Davis was regaining his lost strength. She was heartbroken, driven by the fear of losing him. But she was also jealous that he was seemingly better. He could leave her and make get her kicked out of the place. She would then live in the streets while he would enjoy the summer with his sons and grandchildren. She would have nothing while he got his everything back.

For her whole life, the nun only knew how to take care of people and look after the helpless. She had no other talent to earn money.

NO! The nun was furious! She couldn't stand to watch as Mr. Davis stepped down the steps. She had to take care of him, so he wouldn't have to suffer anymore! He needed someone to look after him... forever!

"Let me help you." Exiting the room under the guise of the caring woman Mr. Davis knew her by, the nun offered to help him, smiling sweetly as always.

"It's fine. I can now move by myself," Mr. Davis replied while moving toward the first step of the stairs. The nun just smiled, assuring him that she would just stay behind for his safety.

Satisfied, Mr. Davis turned toward the stairs, preparing to step down. He moved his leg down the first step, with his cane supporting him as he descended slowly. Just as he was about to make the next step, he suddenly felt his cane being swept away! Mr. Davis soon found himself on his two feet, panicked as he was stuck at the first step. He hung onto the railing, frightened by the sudden force. As he looked up, his eyes shot wide open, overcome with shock.

There, standing above him, a shadowy figure loomed. His heart shrank even more seeing this ghostly image stare at him with wicked eyes. The figure tapped the cane on her hand, looking at Mr. Davis like he was a little mouse.

The man wanted to call for help, but the nun was quick to strike. In one push, the woman threw Mr. Davis down the stairs. His eyes held horror as he flew into the air and started rolling down the steps. He was overcome with so much pain that he could barely move or call for help.

Click clack, click clack! Footsteps were coming towards him. The nun then bent down and gave him a wicked grin. His eyes began to close as he was losing consciousness. Before closing his eyes, he saw her bending down...... and she whispered, "Sorry."

He was soon engulfed by darkness. After a night of screaming and alarm, the nun found herself back in the home. Mr. Davis was admitted to the hospital, where they revealed that he was too injured to walk. The fall was brutal and cruel to his old body; it made it paralyzed along one side. Everyone was sad, of course. For the nun, however, it was just as she wanted.

Now, Mr. Davis would forever need her help. She would not lose him or her place in the home again...

Then, the nun received a call that another patient was arriving. When the old lady was given to her, the nun gave her a welcoming smile. But as she took her in, there was nothing but a seething grin...

Ah, yes... another patient to keep... forever...

Forgotten by The Campfire

Anna might not be the healthiest girl, but she sure was the happiest. The girl knew she had little time, so she used it to hide her pain beneath her smiling face.

Yes, Anna was suffering from leukemia. She didn't fully understand what it meant, but Anna feel that whatever it was, it wasn't good. Forced to live with this condition until she could be healed, Anna lived in a caretaking facility, where they did their best to treat her and other kids suffering from serious medical conditions.

The nurses always checked on her, treating her as she lay in bed. They were all friendly and caring, never leaving her afraid. However, there was only one nurse who Anna loved the most. Miss Sara was a motherly woman who cared for Anna like she was her own child.

Sara would come with a doll and storybook to make Anna's nights much better. She understood Anna like no one else; it made the little girl never ask for anyone else to take care of her other than Sara.

One day, Anna was super excited. Her birthday was a day later, and she wanted something very special to celebrate with her friends and teachers at the care center. Then, she decided what she wanted to do and with whom to share her idea.

"Miss Sara! Miss Sara!" Anna happily cheered. "Can we go on a picnic on the outskirts with all my friends and teachers for my birthday?"

"That's a great idea, Anna. I will tell your plan to the others and let you know their decision, okay? But I can't promise joining you on the trip. I have an urgent errand to run."

Anna's heart dropped, filled with worry. She had gained many friends during her time in the caretakers' facility, and she had grown to like her other teachers. But she could never celebrate without her most caring teacher.

"But... it's my birthday! You have to come!" Anna begged, pulling at Miss Sara's pants. "Please!"

Sara hated to see the girl so sad, knowing she deserved all the happiness in the world. But she had some urgent work and needed to finish things. Choosing between her own deeds and Anna's was a challenge, for sure. Once again, Sara sighed, "I'll try my best."

"No!" Anna cried, not satisfied with her answer. "You have to *promise* me you will come!"

Defeated, Sara turned to Anna and said, "All right, I promise."

"Thank you, Miss Sara!" Anna hugged the caretaker. Sara would do as much as she could to make her happy.

The next day Anna was finally ten. The care center had arranged a bus to take her and her friends on a trip. She was overjoyed. Oh, the fun she could have with her friends, the things she could learn and show the teachers. Most of all, she couldn't wait to spend time with Miss Sara.

It was an hour's travel to their destination. The kids arrived at the field of grass Anna had been talking about. It was a lovely series of hills close to the mountains. Birds were chirping, and the sounds of the river flowing made it the perfect spot to relax in and play about.

As the kids ran out, Anna looked around. To her disappointment, Miss Sara was nowhere to be seen. Anna was confused and worried. Miss Sara promised she would be there. Where was she? The little girl could not tell, but she continued to hope.

The kids played jump rope, chased each other around, and went on a scavenger hunt. Anna waited for Miss Sara to come, but she still wasn't anywhere to be seen.

Heartbroken, Anna finally went to the others. At night, she shared a tent with her two friends, Emily and Rose. Though she cried about Miss Sara's absence, Anna refused to talk about it to her two friends, despite their insistence. They eventually gave up, leaving Anna to weep the night away.

At midnight, the kids and the teachers were all sound asleep... except Anna. She was shivering cold, even covered with a blanket. So, she left the tent quietly and walked to a rock close to the river. There, she sat down, wondering where Miss Sara was and why she had not come. She sobbed and sobbed, heartbroken over the broken promise.

Suddenly, she heard a noise. Anna jumped as her heart beat faster. Was it a wild animal or a friend playing a prank? She couldn't move an inch, too scared to move. Then, out of the trees, she saw *her*... Her eyes watered with tears, and her heart was soothed by warmth.

"Miss Sara!" Anna ran as fast as she could towards Miss Sara. At last, she had finally come! She stopped, seeing Miss Sara covered in dirt and sweat. What had happened to her? Anna was filled with worry. But Miss Sara flashed the same smile she always did. Sara appeared to be a little pale, but Anna thought it was the moonlight that made her glow.

"I kept my promise, didn't I?" Sara asked with a playful smile, in an angelic voice.

Although she was a little too late, Anna couldn't care less. Miss Sara was here, and she had kept her promise. So, the two then spent the night talking about the day. Anna was sad, of course, but she told Sara that she was happy she had come at the end. Sara, in return, was grateful that Anna had enjoyed the day.

After what seemed like hours, the two finally decided to head back to camp. Miss Sara put Anna into the tent, where she would finally sleep peacefully. Before Anna could close her eyes, Miss Sara came over to her ear and said, "Good night, Anna. I will always be with you." She hugged the little girl before leaving.

Anna was confused about why she would say that, but eventually, she slept off...

The next day, everyone was getting ready to head back home. Anna looked around for Miss Sara, hoping to catch a ride with her. But, to her confusion, she wasn't there. She had also noticed Emily and

Rose glancing at her from time to time weirdly and wondered what the matter was.

"Did I do something?" Anna finally decided to confront Emily.

"Umm...no...I mean...yes." Emily hesitated while avoiding eye contact.

Something was definitely wrong.... Anna wondered.

"I saw you yesterday night sitting by the lake and talking to yourself." Rose confronted Anna and spilled the truth.

"What? That can't happen because I was with Miss Sara." Anna replied confidently, yet deep inside, she was shocked by Rose's words.

"No, you weren't. You were all alone. I saw it with my own eyes," Rose said while Emily tried to stop her from getting into an argument.

Before Anna could argue, one of the teachers came by. She then croaked the words everyone dreaded hearing after a peaceful day. Yesterday, Miss Sara had passed away.

Everyone was horrified. A car accident took her life on her way to the campsite. The kids cried, and the teachers grieved at losing one of their most cherished friends. But Anna did not say anything. To her, it felt like time had stopped.

She was driven with more grief and shock than anyone. She was almost about to cry endlessly over the death of her beloved caretaker. But then, after she had wept, she noticed something was off.

Anna then asked the teachers when and how Miss Sara had died. They said she died around eight to nine o'clock at night yesterday. *But how's that possible?* Miss Sara was with her at midnight after she was said to have died. Then... who was with Anna that night?

Anna was so bewildered and confused until she remembered something "Miss Sara" had said.

"I kept my promise, didn't I?"

It was at this point that Anna realized that Miss Sara *did* come... but as a ghost. Knowing that Miss Sara's spirit came to see her made Anna very sad. However, after some time, she was assured that Miss Sara would always be with her, just as she had said for the very last time.

The Birthday Clown

It was Emma's fifteenth birthday, and she was overjoyed! She could hardly control her excitement while sitting in the back of the family car. On both sides were her brother and sister, Jack and Lily. Her parents were in the front, her dad at the wheel.

The family was on a supermarket trip to prepare for her birthday party. They had invited some relatives and Emma's friends in the evening, so they needed to get enough snacks, drinks, and maybe a few decorations.

They stopped at the supermarket, rolling a cart ready to do some shopping. Emma and Jack were asked to fetch some snacks while her parents and her little sister, Lily, fetched some decoration items. After getting the list of things they needed, Emma and Jack walked through the supermarket, picking out the foods and drinks to serve at the party. The siblings filled up most of their list, from soft drinks to candies.

Jack suddenly had the urge to go to the bathroom as soon as they were done. The two of them looked around for the nearest restroom. They then asked one of the shop staff where they could find one. The worker told them that all their bathrooms were undergoing maintenance.

"What?!" Jack yelled in panic. "There must be somewhere I can go!"

"Well... we do have our staff bathroom for emergencies. It's at the back of the store," the worker replied somewhat hesitantly, "but..."

Jack interrupted the worker as he couldn't wait any longer. He ran past her and headed straight for the staff room. Emma sighed before following her brother.

The back of the building was completely empty. The rooms were without workers, leaving the building almost vacated. The computers weren't on, and dust was collecting in many places. All there was to light the room was a single ceiling bult. But that light was flickering on and off, making the room feel even creepier. Emma felt shivers as the space had a horror movie vibe.

Jack quickly rushed to the bathroom, leaving Emma all alone. She looked around, noticing how eerie the atmosphere was; it was making her suffocate. As she kept the basket, she thought to use the other washroom quickly before Jack had returned.

Once she was done, Emma exited the room. She saw her brother playing with a clown mask.

"Where did you get that mask?" Emma asked.

"I just found it in the basket," Jack confirmed. But he suddenly asked her back, "Did you get it for the party?"

Emma shook her head, perplexed by Jack's question. She strictly remembered not putting a clown mask in the basket. Then, Emma found a piece of paper in the basket. One side was blank, while the other had a note printed on it: **Every birthday party needs a birthday clown!**

It was such a strange coincidence that a birthday message happened during her birthday. Either way, Emma didn't seem to care and decided to just throw away the mask and paper. She and Jack returned to their parents with their goodies.

As they got closer to home, Emma looked out the window, thinking she would throw the best party ever. She watched the trees pass by when the car stopped at a red light. Suddenly, Emma saw something by the road. Or rather, *someone...*

At the side of the road was a clown dressed in a yellow suit with polka dots. He had the trademark red nose and creepy makeup. He was staring right at her with a red-lipped grin. On his hand was a blue balloon floating above him.

Looking back at the clown, she saw his eyes... *flash*. Suddenly, Emma's father turned toward her.

"Emma, is there anything you'd like?"

Emma then turned toward her father. But, for some reason, she responded with a bizarre request, "A birthday clown...."

"What?" Her father was clueless, surprised by her answer. Apparently... so was Emma.

Realizing what she had said, Emma shook her head and told him that she was just joking. However, deep inside, she felt very weird about her sudden response. Was she focused so much on that clown by the road that she simply said she wanted one? That was probably it. As to who that clown was, she thought it could be someone doing his job.

Finally, it was evening and Emma was eagerly waiting for everyone to arrive. Her party was fully prepped, and the cake was almost ready. However, her parents had an emergency call at the hospital. As both were surgeons, they had to rush to the hospital, promising to return as soon as possible.

After some time, Emma's friends began to arrive one by one, filling the house with a lively crowd. Emma started the party without delay, treating her friends with food and drinks. She was chatting and giggling with her friends when Jack came over with the cake.

"Mom and Dad will be back home soon," he announced. Emma got more excited... until Jack added, "You're lucky to have your wish fulfilled. The birthday clown is here."

Suddenly, Emma was caught off guard. She asked Jack what he meant by that, and he pointed toward the empty kitchen. She saw the most shocking sight of all. There, in her own kitchen was the same clown she had seen on the road! Standing right in the center with his creepy smile and weird eyes.

Emma grew frightened. How could this be? She had just seen this random clown on the road, far from home. And now, he had just showed up in her kitchen? She was about to tell Jack that she didn't want one when she saw how excited Jack was at seeing the clown. He had always loved clowns and their playful tricks, which made Emma feel conflicted.

Slowly, her friends started piling up behind her, seeing the clown smiling creepily at them all. Everyone was in awe, laughing at his weird look. Seeing her friends so happy, Emma shook off her worry and started getting happy about having the clown around.

She would call her parents to thank them for inviting the clown. However, before she could call them, the clown turned around and started walking toward the backdoor. Everyone was confused, wondering where he was going. Before he could open the door, he turned his head towards the children, grinning wickedly.

One look at him and everyone started to follow him outside. Jack, Lily, Emma, and all the other kids walked out of the backdoor and toward the forest in a line while the clown led the way just a few steps ahead. They were about to leave behind the light coming from Emma's house and walk into the dark forest when...

BRRRINGGG!!!

Emma was suddenly snapped out of her daze only to find that she was no longer at home...She felt her phone vibrating and saw that her mother was calling her. Relieved, she quickly answered the call.

"Hello?" she greeted.

"Honey," her mother responded. "We are on our way back home. How's the party?"

Still confused, Emma wanted to ask her mom about the clown. She felt something was off about the clown and where she was, so she had to know.

"Mom, did you or dad happen to invite a birthday clown?"

"No, honey. We thought you were joking about that," Emma's mother confirmed. The little girl's hand shook; her heart was racing with fear as she realized that the clown was never a part of the plan. Alerted by what she felt, Emma told her mom about the clown. Immediately, her mother fell into panic mode.

"Honey! Listen! Take everyone and get in the house before locking the doors!" she warned. "We are on our way!"

After ending the call, Emma was frightened by her mother's voice. If the clown was that suspicious, then she was terrified. She ran ahead and shook her friends. One by one, the kids all snapped out of their trance and were quickly led out of the forest.

Somehow, the clown and his horrifying toothy grin were nowhere to be seen...

When she returned home, Emma's parents were already there. She immediately went for a hug before telling them what had happened.

Days later, the news broke out about the incident. It led to the startling discovery that several kids had disappeared not long ago. CCTV footage from someone's house revealed that some children had walked away from their houses.

Leading them from their safe house to the deep, dark forest was the same clown with the same frightening grin. Whatever he did to put them in a trance, he had led them straight into the woods, where they were never seen again...

The Haunted Snowman

During one snowy winter season, as Christmas came closer, Joe and his family took a trip up the mountain, hoping to catch the joy away from the city's bustling life. At the top of the winter wonderland, the family found a nice private cabin made of wood — a cozy place where Joe could rest and have fun next to a warm fire.

The place wasn't entirely crowded, making it a quiet spot to stay in. Joe could hardly keep himself from jumping for joy, as this was his first time in a cabin like this. The nearest cabin was around ten to fifteen minutes away on foot, but it was close enough.

After settling in for the night, Joe woke up the following day, taking his little sister Sophie to play outside. Watching the fields so white with snow, the little girl had one easy idea. Of the many games they could play in the snow, Sophie immediately went with the one they both liked the most.

"Let's make a snowman!" she cheered him on.

Being the bigger brother, Joe agreed and went to pile up the snow, rolling up enough. Sophie stood at the building site, waiting impatiently for Joe to bring in the snowballs needed. One by one, Joe placed the snowballs on top of each other to build the snowman.

Finally, after finishing up, the two looked at the completed snowman, checking on their proud work. And it looked...very bland. Their snowman was not so much a snowman as just a white ball. It needed more than just snow. It needed features to make it stand out more - things to make it more... *alive.*

"It could use arms," Sophie commented.

"And eyes and a nose," Joe added. After thinking it through, he had an idea. turning to Sophie, said, "I'm going to look for some things to make its face. Why don't you go find a scarf and some branches for the hands?"

"Okay!" After Sophie ran off to find the things he had asked for, Joe walked to the cabin to find some props. He searched the bags for anything to use, but nothing seemed to work. There was nothing round to make the eyes wide enough, make the mouth long, or light enough to make the nose. There was nothing useful for a snowman's face.

So, Joe exited the cabin, looking for anything outdoors to use for his snowman. As he was searching, he noticed a cabin his parents had driven past the previous day. His curiosity was piqued. Perhaps something in the cabin could be useful for the snowman. So, Joe made his choice, determined to make the ten-minute walk.

As he arrived, Joe got a closer look at the cabin down the hill. He thought he would make some new friends or find things to do. But, to his disappointment, the cabin was not as it had seemed from afar. It was small compared to theirs and looked very shabby, with wooden walls chipped and piled with snow. The gate and doors into the cabin had been left open, revealing the dark inside. The place was clearly abandoned, given that no one appeared to be anywhere.

Joe was about to walk away from the abandoned cabin. Then, out of nowhere, a creaking sound was heard. He turned around and saw the door opening by itself, probably due to the wind. Taking a look into the cabin, Joe suddenly had another idea. Since no one was living there anymore, maybe he could find the needed things for the snowman inside. He decided to turn back and walk toward the cabin.

Opening the creaky door, he entered a dark hallway, where furniture was filled with dust, while the corners of the house were covered in cobwebs. Bits of snow found their way into the house, making it look more abandoned.

Suddenly, Joe's nose picked up a foul smell in the air, causing him to reel. Curious, he followed the scent down to the basement, walking on the creaky steps. Within the basement were shelves with jars left to collect dust. He couldn't see what was in them, so he looked closer.

Jar after jar, he found nothing good. Everything was just old, expired liquids or contents, suggesting they had been there for a long time. The contents looked very disgusting, making him leave behind a lot of them.

Suddenly, as he looked on, he came across a jar that nearly spooked him. Inside was a pair of eyes floating in liquid; they looked very real. Looking closer, Joe felt that he had found just what he needed. He opened the jar and with disgust took them, thinking of using them for the snowman.

Joe quickly looked into the kitchen and snagged a rotten carrot. It wasn't good to eat anymore, so why not make it a nose? After his search was done, Joe ran back to finish the snowman.

When he had returned, Sophie had already gave the snowman branches for its arms, stones for the mouth, and a scarf around its neck. Joe put the carrot and eyes on the face, finally completing the look. When the two looked at it, Joe felt very proud of the snowman. However, Sophie was quiet, creeped out by the eyes, thinking they looked too real.

Soon, the two were done with the snowman and moved on to do other things, leaving their work to stand in the snow... alone.

Later that night, everyone went to sleep to rest for the next day. Joe slept beside a window, covered up nicely under a warm blanket. Suddenly, he felt a sudden chill hit him, waking him up. When he looked at the window, he saw that it was open. Joe could have sworn that it had been closed a while ago. He got up and went to close it, looking at Sophie sleeping peacefully in the other bed.

Joe was about to close the window when he spotted the snowman they had made outside. The last time he remembered, the snowman was looking away from the cabin. Now, to Joe's surprise, it was looking toward the window... Or more like toward him *with cold, human-like eyes.*

Since when did it turn around? Did someone move it? Either way, Joe was very disturbed by how the eyes were looking at him. So, he closed the window and shut the curtains, leaving the snowman to stare...

The next morning, Joe went out to check the snowman. Much to his shock, the snowman was now looking away from the cabin again! While he was more confused than shocked, he decided to let it go, thinking he might be mistaken, and went about his day.

Night came again, and Joe was in bed. He wanted to go to the bathroom, so he got up. After being done with it, he looked out the window again. The snowman was looking back at the cabin again. Its eyes only looked at him, and his smile made Joe shiver.

Terrified of the snowman, Joe closed the curtains and ran to bed. That night, he barely got any sleep.

And sure enough, the next day, the snowman was back in its original position. Joe, feeling very tired and horrified, grabbed his head in terror. He was too scared to tell his parents or Sophie because he didn't want to ruin their vacation. Too afraid to sleep alone, he asked his parents if he could sleep in the unused room, which had no windows at all. Joe lied that it was too cold to sleep in the other room. Although they were curious, they agreed to let him sleep in that room.

Finally, at night, Joe was all alone, with no windows and, thus, no snowman to bother him. He tucked himself in bed, hoping to get a good night's sleep at last. Suddenly, Joe was awakened by the same chill that had come over before. However, it was now even colder, almost like he was sleeping in the snow. Overcome by frost and fear, Joe could not move, and his body grew numb. As he tried to break free, he looked at the door. What he saw made his body shiver even more...

At the door was the same snowman, now standing in his room. Staring at Joe with its frightening eyes, it slid toward Joe. The boy tried to move or scream, but his mouth was frozen, unable to speak. The snowman got closer and closer until its branch arms moved to grab the boy. Its stony mouth turned into an evil grin, with its eyes glowing red. Joe couldn't move or scream; he was slowly losing consciousness.

He woke up after a few hours and found his family gathered around his bed.

"W-Where is the snowman!?" Joe asked in horror. In confusion, they told him/

"What snowman, honey?" his mother replied.

Joe told them what had happened; but to his surprise, there was no snowman. Sure enough, when he went outside, the snowman was no longer there; he was completely gone.

After being shrouded in fear, Joe decided he had had enough. Thankfully, the family was ready to leave the cabin. As soon as they had checked out, the receptionist asked if Joe was all right, noticing his sickly look.

When his parents told what had happened, the lady... also froze. She then told them that a few years ago, a couple rented the abandoned cabin Joe had entered earlier. A few days later, they went missing, and no one had seen them since. Since then, people have considered the cabin to be haunted.

Joe, now more terrified than ever, knew he wasn't dreaming. That night, he had seen what horrors were to be found up the mountain. He now knew that the items he took from the cabin caused a curse to attack him. From that day forth, he stopped going to abandoned places all by himself, never to face such dark things again...

The Girl in the Hotel

Oliver and his family were home from vacation when their car broke down. It was a stormy night, so there was no help around. Stuck without any way out, the family then spotted something on the map. A hotel nearby could be seen over the horizon. They decided to make the walk, which would take about ten minutes.

As the family came toward the hotel, they found that it was not very comforting. The building was in a poor state, having been left in the dirt, and there were very few visitors. However, the family was content with it since they would have a roof over their heads while they found a repairman to fix the car.

Upon entering to check in for the night, they went up to the receptionist. She was a kind lady who gave Oliver a few candies as a welcome gift. The receptionist then gave them the room key for the night. Before they could go check the room, the receptionist stopped them with a glum look.

"Do not go to the floor above yours," she warned as if she were a security guard. "Some repairs are being done upstairs." Oliver and his parents heeded the warning. However, Oliver felt that the warning was a little weird. The building definitely needed repairs, but how she warned them had him worried.

In the end, Oliver and his family went up and entered the room. The room wasn't too bad, even if a bit dirty. The beds were clean enough, so Oliver needn't be worried about sneezing from the dust. Soon, the family was ready to go to bed. Oliver would sleep on the bed next to his parents.

As he drifted off, he suddenly felt a chilly sensation. He woke up feeling colder than usual. The fan wasn't that strong, so it couldn't have made it so chilled. He looked around, wondering what was freezing him.

But there was nothing...

Then, out of nowhere, he felt a tap on his right shoulder. He looked to the right and saw that his parents were still asleep. Then, another tap. Oliver turned to his left...

"Hello!" A girl popped out of nowhere!

Before Oliver could scream, the girl quickly covered his mouth, stopping him from making any noise.

"Shush! Not so loud!" the girl whispered. Oliver panicked for a little before calming himself down. He looked at the girl, thinking she was about his age. She wore a yellow dress and had her hair tied into two buns. Wait! How did she even get inside?

"Who are you and how did you get in here?" asked Oliver. The girl gave him a sheepish smile before replying, "You didn't lock your door."

Oliver got out of bed and looked at the door. To his surprise, it was indeed open. That was weird, he thought. Didn't his parents lock the door? He specifically remembered hearing his mother lock it.

"I saw the door wide open, so I had to check it out," the girl added. After some awkward silence, the girl sighed, "I'm bored. Let's go play!" Oliver couldn't tell if she was serious or not. How could he possibly think about playing games so late at night, with his parents sleeping no less?

He hesitated, not wanting to wake his parents up. However, the girl looked eager and excited, so Oliver felt bad about turning down her offer. Finally, after some thought, he agreed. Satisfied, the girl took his hand and dragged him out. Oliver was a little worried, but he thought that a girl his age wouldn't think about hurting him in any way.

After they closed the door, the girl skipped around the corridor. Oliver would have told her to stay quiet if the hotel didn't have so few people. She stopped in front of him and extended her hand. "I am Mia Smith!"

Oliver reluctantly took the hand and shook it.

"I'm Oliver," he greeted. "So, what are you doing here?"

"Oh, my family and I were here on vacation," Mia explained before she huffed disappointingly. "But I really hate this place. It's so... so lame!" Then, her face softened, looking very sad. "And it gets really lonely here."

Oliver couldn't understand why anyone would feel lonely, especially since she had her parents with her. However, he didn't say anything, thinking his question would be pointless.

"You don't have any friends to play with?" Oliver asked.

"In this place? There are no other kids here," Mia explained. "That leaves you and me!"

Suddenly, Oliver saw Mia perk up. She turned to him and grabbed his hands again.

"Let's go upstairs!" she suggested. To this, Oliver backed away.

"We shouldn't!" he warned. "The old lady said we shouldn't go there." Yet, Mia kept assuring him that everything was going to be fine.

"Come on! I've been there!" she insisted. "There's no one up here to repair the floor anyway!"

Oliver was unsure if Mia was telling the truth. The old lady had seemed serious about the floor above being under repair. However, Mia couldn't possibly be lying, or could she? So, Oliver couldn't say no and agreed to follow her.

When they got up there, Oliver found that the floor, much like the one below him, was still intact. It didn't seem too badly damaged apart from a few cracks on the wall. The floor itself was also safe, and it did look empty. Mia then ran towards one of the rooms and called for Oliver.

"Let's play some hide-and-seek!" she offered. Oliver was still scared of the emptiness of the room, but Mia held his hand again. With one look at Mia's sweet smile, he felt his fears vanish, somewhat thankful that someone wanted to play with him.

And so, having nothing to fear, Oliver agreed, going off with Mia in their game of hide-and-seek. The two played for hours, having a blast hiding from room to room. Never had Oliver have so much fun playing with someone his age. Mia was just full of fun and energy! How had he missed so much? He didn't want to stop playing!

They played and played until Oliver let out a strong yawn. Seeing him yawn, Mia came to him and said, "Maybe we should get you back to bed."

Oliver didn't want to go to bed, but his body was slowing down and his eyes were shutting. Reluctantly, he allowed Mia to lead him back to his room. There, he and Mia looked at each other before he could go in.

"Thank you for playing with me. And also, for the candies. I've had fun after such a long time," Mia said with her eyes twinkling in happiness.

Oliver smiled, thankful that a kid like Mia had fun with him. Alas, with another yawn, Oliver was about to sleep. Before they parted ways, Mia gave Oliver a high-five, confirming their friendship. She then turned around and left him, disappearing into the corridor.

Oliver couldn't look away from Mia for a while, so happy for the fun he had had.

The next day, Oliver woke up and decided to sneak upstairs to find Mia. He looked around for her, but to his sadness, he couldn't find her. He called to her, but her voice could not be heard.

Then, he looked into one of the rooms for Mia. There at an opened window, he saw what looked like a bracelet. On that bracelet, it read the name, "Mia Smith". Grabbing the bracelet, Oliver then went down to find her. At the reception counter, Oliver ran to meet the old lady. She saw the boy and smiled.

"And what can I do for you?" she asked. Oliver then put the bracelet on top of the counter, which the old lady took. After she read the bracelet's tag, her heart stopped. Oliver noticed that her face grew frightened. She covered her mouth and sighed before telling him,

"I'm sorry, dear," she said. Oliver was clueless. Why was she apologizing? Did something happen to Mia?

Turned out, what the old lady said next was... something *had already* happened...

Mia Smith was a guest in the hotel. She was with her family on vacation, just as she had said. They lived on the floor where Oliver had played with her. But then, one night, Mia was sleepwalking toward an open window when suddenly, she fell out of it.

Oliver gasped in horror, learning that Mia had died instantly after the brutal fall. But how could that be?! If Mia was dead, then who did he play with last night? He was distraught in disbelief that the girl he had so much fun with wasn't really there at all. Could it have been a dream? Or was it... Mia's ghost?

Oliver had little time to ask for more answers. The repairman had finished repairing their car, and he didn't want to scare his parents. So, with the mystery deep in his head, Oliver was forced to leave without asking anything more.

The car then drove off, leaving the haunted hotel behind. Oliver looked back at the building and saw someone at the top of it. From that same window, he saw the image of the same girl he had seen last night. The little girl, Mia Smith, was standing at the window, waving at him.

And before Oliver could call for his mother, in a blink, Mia disappeared into thin air....out of his sight and *maybe* out to find her next playmate.

Billie Lost His Boo!

In a huge mansion was a family of three, thrilled about living in a large, impressive house. Cole was happy that his parents decided to move into an extravagant castle that he could only dream of.

The mansion was beyond anything he could have ever imagined when he had first seen it. He love to run around the large yard and the many rooms in the house. Most of all, he loved the view from the terrace, gazing at the big city and its bright lights.

But as soon as he tried to get up there, his mother sat him down and warned him to stay away from the third floor. Apparently, the mansion was too old, and the third floor needed some repairs before settling in. Disappointed, Cole had no choice but to listen, not wanting to cause any trouble.

One day, having spent a month at the mansion, Cole was playing while whistling on the second floor. At that moment, his parents were away at work while their helper, Mrs Taylor, was downstairs in the kitchen.

Suddenly, as he was walking the stairs, he heard a faint whistle echoing down the floors. Cole was spooked by the sudden sound, wondering if it was just the wind. Then, he heard it again. It now sounded like an actual whistle. He looked around and wondered where it had come from. Clearly, it was not his parents as they had gone to work early in the morning, and neither was it Mrs Taylor, who was busy preparing the dinner meal.

So, who could it be? Cole was curious to know. Despite his parents telling him not to go up, he could not resist checking it out. Then, a third whistle came. Finally, Cole made a decision. He went up the steps for the first time, following the sounds to the third floor.

When Cole got to the third floor, he found himself in an empty hallway; the walls had cracks, and the floor were filled holes. It almost looked like the floor could crumble down at any moment. Yet, Cole pressed on making creaking sounds while following more of the whistles. He continued until the very end of the hallway, where he found one of the doors slightly open. Cole headed for the door and looked into it.

Suddenly, a gust of wind blew past him, sending a chill down his spine. As the cold lingered, he heard the screeching sound of a cupboard door opening. Taking a deep breath, Cole prepared to open the door. When he pulled it back, there within the dark room he saw a smaller kid looking away, shivering. The kid didn't look at Cole; he seemed scared.

Cole called out to the boy, "Who are you? What are you doing in our house?"

The boy turned toward Cole, clearly showing his fear. He stood up nervously, twiddling his thumbs. He then answered, "M-My name is Billie."

"What are you doing here?" asked Cole again. Billie took a while to answer before he spoke. "I was just... trying to be scary."

Cole nearly laughed. How could this kid try to be scary if he had been found cowering on the floor? Billie then talked again, still nervous.

"You see... I... I..."

Suddenly, Cole's eyes grew big. He laid his eyes on Billie, watching the little, timid boy... *float*! The boy then moved his hands around, causing the door behind Cole to close without anyone there. Several chairs moved around the room, flying around Cole like crows in the sky, scaring him even more.

When the sudden power show was done, Billie landed on the ground before looking at Cole and *shyly* speaking, "I am a ghost."

Cole could hardly speak, slapping himself to make sure he wasn't dreaming. He wasn't scared only surprised. He was shocked to see tricks only seen in movies and cartoons. Then, he turned around and took another good look at the ghostly kid. Ghosts were supposed to be scary and deadly, right?

Coming closer to Billie, he asked, "Why are you here?"

"I... um..." Billie was quite shy, unable to answer properly. "I can't scare people."

"Scare people? You mean make them tremble like we see in movies?" Cole asked.

"Yeah. The ghostly overlords said I wasn't scary enough, so they put me here until I could be scarier." Billie added as he trailed further into the room. Then, he suddenly turned and flew toward Cole, trying to spook him.

Cole, however, remained still. Then, his frown turned into a smile. Finally, he burst into laughter, finding Billie's attempt more amusing than scary. Saddened, Billy slinked back onto the floor, moping from his failed attempt.

Once Cole had stopped laughing, he looked at the poor ghost, feeling sorry for him. He bent down and asked Billie why the "ghostly overlords" had banished him from their ghost world.

Billie then told Cole that he was supposed to be on a mission. He was sent there to scare ten humans in order to earn his place in the world of the undead. However, he could not bring himself to be scary, as he was quite a weak little boy when alive, always frightened by the slightest noise.

Cole understood how the boy felt. Suddenly, he had the urge to help this ghost achieve his mission. Sure, he was a ghost, but he was a ghost who needed a human's help. And so, Cole took Billie with him and snuck him downstairs to his room.

For the next few days, Cole and Billie sat together and watched horror movies, hoping to teach Billie how to truly frighten a human. However, before they could even reach half the first movie, Billie couldn't watch anymore, frightened by the numerous scenes of monsters and ghosts jumping onto the screen and scaring him. Billie would close his eyes in terror while Cole, on the other hand, just laughed.

As Billie calmed down, Cole would show him how these movies scare people and that the important thing was to come at your target when they least expect it.

"That is what you call a 'jump scare'," Cole said. Billie took note and learned how to jump scare others.

Billie would find an easy target for his first test, one who would shriek at the sight of his ghostly image. Cole, to his amusement, chose none other than Mrs Taylor. While Mrs Taylor was covered in a mask, applying some kind of beauty product on her face, the two boys got ready to spring their trap. Just when she was about to relax, the ghost got in front of the lady.

But as he looked at her, Billie screamed, "Aaahhh!!!", terrified by the ugly mask she was wearing. He ran, leaving Cole to sigh and Mrs Taylor to wonder who was screaming.

The next day when they tried again, Billie accidentally stepped on a toy brick, hurting himself. Though Billie was disappointed, Cole assured him that there was still hope.

"You know what you're missing?" asked Cole. "You're missing your Boo."

"My Boo?" asked Billie.

"The sound ghosts make. You need to have your own Boo!" To Billie, this made sense. Every ghost he had watched made this scary sound that frightened him. And so, the kids tried again the next day. The kids were playing catch while planning their next trick when they heard a scream coming from the floor downstairs. Cole had just passed the ball to Billie as he peeked down and saw Mrs Taylor staring at him with wide eyes. Her lips trembled, and her eyes slowly moved to Billie, who was invisible to her.

Billie then remembered that he made himself invisible when not scaring others. For all they knew, Mrs Taylor saw a ball float around.

Oh... now, there was an idea...

Cole whispered to Billie and told him to wave the ball around Mrs Taylor. Moving the ball here and there, the ghost was finally making this helper shake in her shoes. When she became even more scared, Billie went in for the final blow.

He made himself visible and yelled, "BOOO!!!"

Mrs Taylor instantly fell to the ground, knocked out by fear. Billie could hardly believe it. He had scored his first scare! Cole gave the ghost a high-five, congratulating him for a job well done.

The next day, Mrs Taylor quit her job without telling Cole's parents the actual reason. She was too embarrassed to call herself a scaredy cat, so the middle-aged woman silently resigned from her job.

Since then, Billie has become braver and more confident with Cole's help. Unfortunately, things turned out for the worse. Cole was told that his family had to move out after his father was transferred to the city. Cole and Billie grew sad, knowing they had to split up.

On the day the family was to leave, Cole had to leave something behind for Billie to help him remember their time together. From out of his wardrobe, Cole gave him some ghost masks from Halloween, along with a three-legged costume he had for his school's costume party. In return, Billie would do his best to be a scary ghost, using the tricks he was taught.

After moving out of the mansion, Cole and his family moved into an apartment in the city. A year later, Cole got word of the old mansion. He heard that the mansion continued to have new people moving in, only for them to run out after experiencing weird and scary things. None lasted long, suggesting that Billie was indeed making himself scarier than before.

With a total of five families out of the mansion, that would definitely make him worthy of the underworld. And for that, Cole was proud, knowing that his new friend would make it...

Stay Away from the Thirteenth Floor

Jack and his mom had recently moved to a new apartment after his parents agreed to a mutual divorce, and the mom got custody. As thrilled as he was to live with his mother and not witness his parents fighting, Jack's excitement was buried when the kid saw how shabby the place looked.

"As soon as I get a job, we'll move out. I promise," the mother assured her kid, who soon became grateful to have a roof above their head.

It was the last day of shifting things, and as Jack finished moving a box, he saw his mother talking to an old lady standing in front of the elevator. Standing while hunching forward, this old lady had a great big smile on her wrinkly face.

"Why don't you come over for some dinner on the weekends, if you have the time?" the old lady offered.

"Oh, we would love to!" Jack's mom thanked her.

After their friendly greeting, Jack and his mom went into the old elevator, pressing the button to ascend towards the 12th floor, where their new home awaited.

A week into the move, Jack tried to settle into the new place, only to be irritated by dust and the lack of air-conditioning. Worst of all, there was no one his age to talk to. His friends were back at his old place, so there was no one to have fun with now.

It was a rainy afternoon, and his mom was out job hunting, leaving Jack all bored and sad. He had to miss school due to the weather and was starting to hate being alone. Picking up a ball, Jack thought to pass the time by playing around, so he went outside into the big, empty hallway. He kicked and bounced until the ball landed in front of the elevator.

Ding.....Jack heard the elevator ring as he came to pick up the ball, meaning someone must be coming his way. He waited for the person to come out, leaving his ball to the side. Then, the doors opened. From within the dirty elevator, there was...

No one?

Jack looked in and found that the elevator had no one inside. He knew that it was almost impossible for an elevator to come up without anyone pressing it. As Jack looked into the elevator, a thought came into his head. He had never ridden an elevator alone before. This was his chance to explore an entire building without his mom's knowledge. She always said that it was dangerous to ride alone as there could be bad people everywhere.

Now, he was all alone. He had the chance to see this big apartment and make new friends. So, he stepped into the elevator right before the doors closed. He viewed the many buttons on the panel, wondering which floor to select.

There were many buttons, and as Jack started to get confused, his eyes fell on a number. It was the only button accessible at his little height, so he clicked on the number 13, making his way to the floor upstairs. The elevator rocked, nearly tripping him before it rose up. One floor later, Jack found himself at his destination. Soon, the doors opened...

Jack looked upon a dark hallway. There dark bloats and cracks all over the floor and walls, with bits of plaster littering the ground. The hall was abandoned, with no one to be seen. All the doors were locked shut... all except one.

At that door, Jack could hear something echoing from the room. It was a humming sound, almost like someone was singing a song.

Curiously, he followed the humming, sneaking quietly on tip toes. He was about to peek in and find out who lived on this shabby floor...until...

"Hello there!"

"AAAHHH!!!" Jack dropped to the floor, frightened by the sight of a scary old man popping out of the door. His wide-open smile seemed creepy on his wrinkly face, making him look like a goblin. Jack breathed heavily as his eyes lay on the creepy man, who exited the room to meet him. With his thin, bent body, he grinned warmly at the boy.

With a cackling laugh, the man approached Jack and helped him. "Why don't you come inside?" The man turned back to his apartment and entered. "No one has ever come up here in so long. It's nice to have some company."

Jack wanted to leave but couldn't say no to a man in need of company. So, he followed him into the room, closing the door shut. Jack then looked around the place, seeing that it was no better than the hallway outside. He sat in a dusty old chair and waited for the man to sit on opposite him. The man came, seeing Jack's nose twitch in disgust.

"The chair smells bad, I know," the man laughed. "Now, what's your name, son?"

"My name's Jack," the boy greeted. "I just moved here a week ago."

"I've lived here for only a few years myself, kid," the man added. "If you forget about the smell, this place is actually pretty good!" Jack found it hard to believe a place as old and rotten as this was "good".

With his hearty laugh, the man continued to tell Jack about his time in his house. In return, Jack found the man quite funny, despite his haggard appearance. Soon, the two shared stories, with Jack telling the old man about his old home.

For hours, the two talked, making each other laugh and enjoy each other's company. Soon, Jack finally found someone whom he could hang out with. The man told him that he should visit every day, and Jack agreed.

Upon returning home, Jack told his mom about the friend he met, making her very happy about him. However, when Jack told her he was an old man, she was surprised and a bit suspicious. But she was glad he was finally opening up to someone. If the old lady was a friendly neighbor, this man could be one too.

That night, as Jack and his mother were asleep, a loud knock was heard, causing the mother to wake up. She checked the clock, seeing that it was three in the morning! Disturbed, she wondered who could be up this late.

As she approached the door, the knocking turned into a loud banging, alarming her into action. She went to the front door, where it knocked and knocked some more. Then, she came to the door and looked through the peephole. When she looked, she found that outside, there was no one...

This confused her. Who could it be? Jack's mom wondered, and when there were no more knocks, she slowly turned to sleep again. But the door knocked again, more violently than before. With a gasp, she ran back and looked into the peephole. Again, there was no one... nothing but an empty, big hallway.

She came to her room in a hurry, seeing that Jack was fast asleep. Giving her child a hug, she retreated to her own bed and fell asleep. The knocking was no more.

The following day, Jack's mom was in a terrible mood, having lost some sleep after the knocking, which had been replaying in her head. As she was ready for breakfast, she saw Jack with a sad face. He then turned to his mom and said, "Mom? Why didn't you let my friend in?"

The mother was clueless. What did Jack mean? Who would come all the way to their apartment at night?

"What do you mean, honey?" she asked, pretending to not be freaked out.

"The old man. He told me that you didn't open the door when he came," Jack said.

At that moment, his mother was scared out of her wits. She recalled seeing no one in the empty hallway, and only the sound of someone knocking was heard. Could the knocking on the door be him? Why would he want to come all the way down to see them? What was that old man thinking?

For now, the mother decided to see if she could see this old man and know what his business was. The next day, as Jack went to school, his mother walked out of the room to find the man on the thirteenth floor. Suddenly, she bumped into the old lady from the nearby room. With her bright smile, she asked where the woman was going. And so, Jack's mom told her she was going to the thirteenth floor to meet the old man who lived there.

Suddenly, the old woman trembled, her face wrecked with fear. With her shaking voice, she then mumbled, "Th-that's impossible. You must be mistaken!"

Jack's mom hardly knew what she was talking and, so she asked, "What? What's wrong?"

The old woman then looked up and asked her with a frightened look. "Does the man have a name?"

Jack's mom didn't have a name, saying that her son only referred to him as his "friend". Overcome with fright, the old lady told a story that Jack's mom could not forget. There was once an old man who lived on the thirteenth floor who hearing problems. One day, the building caught on fire and spread to the thirteenth floor. The fire alarm rang as loud as it could, warning all who lived there... except the old man.

The deaf old man couldn't hear the alarm ringing, so he sat there, seemingly unaware of the blaze... until it was too late. After the old man burned to death, the owner of the building declared to demolish the entire thirteenth floor, leaving it abandoned and destroyed. That was why the building is said to have twelve floors.

The old lady's story frightened Jack's mom. So, an old man died on a floor that was supposed to be empty and abandoned? Alarmed, she ran into the elevator and found no button to the thirteenth floor!

She returned to her home and looked up the incident on the thirteenth floor. She found a picture of the old man who had died, scaring her even more. At that moment, Jack returned from school and saw his mother looking at a picture. As he walked closer, his face grew confused when he uttered something shocking.

"Why are you looking at my *friend's* photo?" Jack asked with a puzzled look.

"Is this the old man you go up to meet?" his mom cautiously asked, trying her best to hide her panic.

And Jack, to her surprise, said yes. Jack's mom panicked in absolute horror, racing to find her things in the room. She had had it! The place was haunted!

The next month, Jack and his mother left the apartment for good, fleeing to the mother's sister's house for a while. The next few days, the news broke out that the apartment building was demolished after neighbors complained about loud noises.

While Jack continued to worry about his lost "friend", his mother was relieved that she was out of that haunted apartment building. Little did she know that Jack's "friend" may not be so far away from home...

The Eleventh Ghost

Halloween was in full swing, and the town was out to do some trick or treating. As kids walked around in costumes, looking for candy, two sisters named Ellie and Emma were ready to take it to the next level.

"Hey, I have an idea!" Emma exclaimed excitedly. "There's a cool new haunted house at the school tonight!"

"Sounds like fun!" Ellie agreed. "What do we get to do?"

"It's said that people are challenged to get inside and explore the place, but people are dressed as ghosts to try and scare guests," Emma explained.

"What kind of ghosts are they going as?" Ellie asked.

"I don't know. But that's why I want to go! Are you coming with me?" asked Emma.

"Of course! Let's go!"

And so, the two sisters went to the school; it was adorned with all kinds of Halloween decorations. The lighting was made dark and creepy, and it glowed through the windows. They both went in, thrilled about being in a haunted house.

Ellie and Emma then saw a poster, showing that the first person to leave the place without being scared will win a cash prize of hundred dollars. Now, even more excited, they both entered the challenge.

When it was their turn, they saw three kids run out screaming like little girls, causing them to giggle. As they got in, they were told that the place was haunted by ten ghosts. If they managed to pass these ghosts, they would win the challenge. The girls nodded, ready to face their fears and make their Halloween super scary.

The bell rang, and the two went in, racing through the hallways. Mist filled the corridors, and webs hung at the corners. The doors and lockers were left open, leaving decorations of pumpkins and skeletons to haunt the halls. As soon as they stepped inside, to their left...

"RRAAARRRGHH!!!"

The first ghost jumped out of the classroom, showing his tongue while shaking his arms around. The costume was definitely a scary one, almost real-looking. However, the girls did not even flinch. They moved on by booing the ghost's scream and sticking their tongues out.

The both of them were soon jumped at by the second ghost that looked like a sea monster filled with seaweed. Next, they came across the third ghost. Then the fourth, and then the fifth...

Ghost after ghost, the girls didn't scream at the sight of any one of them. The eighth ghost, a zombie, did make Emma yelp a bit, but

Ellie was quick to give her sister some courage, allowing them to move on.

Finally, the girls reached the tenth room. After they went in, they were met with a powerful scream by a sheet of white, with a giant scary face and one eye blown over it. Yet, even with this final force, the girls didn't scream.

With the tenth ghost overcome, the sisters walked out of the tenth room, feeling victorious. They had overcome all the ghosts and were one step closer to winning the cash prize. The sisters walked to the exit, excited to grab the cash prize for their win. But as they were about to exit, Ellie turned around, finding that Emma had stopped to look at another passage. She went to her sister and asked her.

"What's wrong, Emma?" Ellie just pointed her finger down the passage, somewhat spooked by something.

"I think I...." Ellie stopped herself, unsure of what to say next.

"What happened?" Emma asked again.

"I think I saw another ghost."

Emma looked at the passage, confused. They said there were ten ghosts for the challenge. Was this a trick? Could there be another challenge to face that the staff didn't tell them about? If that was the case, then maybe there was a better prize awaiting!

"Well, let's go find out!" Emma cheered.

"But... we already beat the challenge," reminded Ellie.

"Come on, sis!" assured Emma. "We have to try it out!"

Ellie hesitated, unsure if they should waste their time in finding another ghost. However, seeing Emma so excited, she was forced to accept the decision. So, the two sisters went to find out if there was an eleventh ghost in these halls. Their adventurous nature took them into a dark room with very little light. The walls were red, looking a lot like blood.

Mustering up their courage, Emma and Ellie walked into the room. However, before they stepped in, they heard a soft, crying noise. They saw a dark figure crouching on the ground right in front of them. It rocked back and forth, moaning with an eerie voice.

Emma and Ellie were a little creeped out, but they braved themselves and entered the room. They then reached out to face the ghost and win an even bigger prize. Then, as they came closer, the ghost turned to them, revealing its horrifying face! For the first time ever, the girls were finally shocked beyond their wildest fears. The face was horrible and bloodied, with bruises and reddened teeth!

The ghost then grabbed Emma's hand, gripping it so tightly. It then screamed at them, wailing, "YOU KILLED ME!!!" it shrieked as loud as a banshee in the night, making the girls scream just as loud. Emma screamed first, and Ellie had to pull her sister out of the grip, causing her wrist to be stained by the ghost's bloodied hand.

As they ran out, the girls headed straight for the exit on the other side. They raced through the long hallway, only to hear the screeching scream of the ghost running toward them! It screamed and screamed, yelling the same words that terrified them.

"YOU KILLED ME! YOU KILLED ME!"

The girls could see the horrifying face of the ghost, scaring them even more. They got closer and closer to the exit, with the ghost about to grab them with its haggard hand! Then, the girls made one last jump, reaching out of the exit to the safety of the outdoors. They turned around to see if the ghost would attack them. But, to their surprise, the ghost was not there. There was just a dark hallway with no one in sight.

Their hearts were beating so much, traumatized by the gruesome sight of a ghost that tried to kill them. They were sweating from head to shoulder, their bodies overcome by tiredness and fright. They had never been so scared in their lives, so horrified that they almost had a heart attack.

As they got up, they heard some laughter coming from the school. They then saw the staff laughing at them. The girls then realized that they had come out frightened and screaming. They had just lost the challenge. Or did they? That ghost was too scary to even be part of a fake haunted house. So, the staff seemed to have played a dirty trick on them. Angered by the staff, they then complained about the eleventh ghost. But, the staff just shrugged their shoulders. They told the girls that there was no eleventh ghost. There were only ten, just as they said them.

The girls tried to convince the staff that they did see a scary witch-like ghost that was bloodied and an absolute monster. They even took the staff to the room where it all had happened. As it turned out, the room they entered was just a storage room. Checking the CCTV footage, the girls could see themselves running across the hallway. But there was no ghost behind them...

How could this be? They clearly saw the ghost together. They couldn't be lying! Emma then tried to show the fingerprints on her wrist from when the ghost had grabbed her... only to find that there were none.

Now, the girls were beyond frightened. The prize money was immediately forgotten. They were completely fearful of the eleventh ghost that had chased them across the hallway. If the staff had no idea about the eleventh one, then that only meant one thing....

They had come across a real ghost!

The One Who Cried Tory

Once upon a time, there lived a girl named Tory, who used to work as a part-time babysitter, taking care of kids for some extra cash. The kids she looked after were two little sisters named Alice and Anna, aged five and six.

Their parents were healthcare workers who worked their shifts all day, forcing them to come back late at night. Tory would usually be called to take care of the two when both parents had to work late. The sisters loved Tory so much that they would call her Big Sissy because she was like the caring big sister they never had. Tory really adored the cute girls for their joyful natures.

One night, Tory had put the kids to sleep. She was walking down the stairs and into the living room. She turned on the TV and waited out the night until the parents came home. She watched a comedy show while lying on the couch to liven up the night. As she was watching, she heard a faint sound, almost like someone was calling out her name.

"...ori...!"

Tory was startled by the noise and lowered the volume to listen out for the sound. She looked around for the noise but found it very hard to see because it was so dark with only the living room being lit.

Then she heard it again! "Tor...i...!"

This time, Tory heard the voice clearer, sounding like a little girl. In fact, the voice sounded like one of the girls upstairs. Tory even believed that the voice belonged to Alice, having played with them long enough to recognize their individual voices.

So, Tory left the living room and walked into the dark hallway leading to the stairs. Although it was a summer's night, goosebumps were appearing on her skin. When she got to the stairs, she called Alice again. Still, no word from the little girl.

Gulping from being scared, Tory then looked into all the other rooms downstairs. After checking every one, she could not find little Alice in any of them. Suddenly, she went to the basement door, and to her surprise, it was open...

Tory felt it was strange. She had seen that it was closed a while ago. Maybe Alice opened the door and went into the basement. She was about to check it out when, again, she heard the same voice....

"Tory...!"

Tory was sure this time. That was definitely Alice calling out to her. She was curious to know why Alice would run into the dark basement so late at night without her knowing. She then went into the basement and called her from up the steps.

"Alice? Are you there?"

Yet again there was no sound, only the echoes of Tory's voice. She decided to go down into the basement to find out if Alice was there.

She reached for the light switch and flicked it on...but it did not turn on. Tory freaked out when the lights did not come on. Was there a power outage? She looked in the direction of the living room and saw a faint light, meaning the TV was still on.

Regardless, Tory moved down the steps, needing to find Alice. Then, she heard her name being called again.

"Tory...!"

This time, the voice sounded frightened. Did Alice somehow sleepwalk into the basement and was now lost in the darkness? As she moved into the basement, Tory kept repeatedly hearing Alice's voice call out to her. But the voice seemed to have moved further and further away. Finally, she was about to get off the last step when she heard Alice again.

"Tory...!"

Tory was about to call Alice again when she froze while realizing a very frightening thought. Since when did Alice call her by her name? The little girl and her sister always called Tory "Big Sissy". Never once did they call her "Tory". So, why would Alice say her real name? This made Tory freeze with fear.

Again, she called out for Alice, still not getting any reply. All she heard was the voice calling her name.

"Tory..."

It kept calling to her with the same pitch and tone, making her feel more and more uneasy. At that point, Tory realized that she was not hearing Alice anymore. Something else was there.

Eventually, the voice got so frightening that Tory eventually decided she had to run. She ran and closed the basement door. She then ran up to check on the kids, searching their room. To her surprise, the kids were right there, fast asleep!

However, that did not get rid of her fear of the voice. Afraid of what it was that called out to her, she closed the door to the kids' room and locked it. She'd then wait outside until the parents returned, hoping that whatever was out there wouldn't hurt the sisters.

When the parents returned, Tory decided not to tell them as she did not know what exactly had haunted her, and she didn't want them to worry. But to ease her mind, she told them she wouldn't be coming for a week because of a school exam.

The next week, when Tory was walking by, she saw that the couple was moving out of the house. She came over to ask them what had happened and learned that after she had left, they felt an ominous presence in the building. It all came down when Anna woke up crying, telling the parents that there was something in the closet, watching them sleep.

When they checked the closet, they found no one. However, they found something more disturbing. Behind the closet were written

words made of claw marks that asked the parents to choose...Anna
or Alice?

The dangerous writing soon convinced the parents that the house
was haunted. Tory was relieved that the family chose to leave the
house; and since the family left, the house was never put on sale
again, but was left to rot, leaving whatever evil was haunting them
all...

The Candy Woman

On a dark, cold night, it was again the spookiest time of the year. Halloween was back, and children were out getting candy while dressed in scary costumes. Among those kids was a group of four trick-or-treaters named Kevin, Noah, Lucy, and Anna. They were dressed as a mummy, a witch, a skeleton, and a phantom. They began making spooky noises to get sweets and candy into their baskets. They used to get many sweets every year, enough to make them full overnight.

This year, however, each basket only had three or four candies when there used to be twelve or more. Kevin took the blame on himself, first and foremost. He had had an accident earlier in the day. After helping his mother carry some boxes, he tripped and fell down the stairs, breaking his arm. He had to stay home in dire pain until they could put a cast over his arm. With his arm injured, he had no choice but to be a not-so-scary mummy while the others wore scarier costumes.

While the others tried not to make Kevin feel bad, he insisted that he was at fault. Disappointed with their score, the group had to walk back home, having lost the Halloween spirit this year. Suddenly, as they walked on, they smelled something delicious! Their noses picked up the savory smell until they found a house in the middle of the suburbs — the most isolated place in the entire town. All around them were a few abandoned houses, except for the one emitting the smell. Noah's stomach rumbled at the smell, making him feel very hungry.

"Maybe we should go check that house?" he suggested. The others were hesitant. They didn't know this part of town or who lived in it. However, when they looked into their empty baskets, their minds changed. Maybe, they should trick-or-treat at this house. Whatever was being cooked in would be worth more than any candy!

The group walked together and entered through the metal gate. The gate opened with a loud, creaking sound. Suddenly, the noise was so loud that a cauldron of bats flew from a dead tree and right for the children. The kids ducked as the bats raced past them, terrifying them. After the bats flew off, the children were calmed by the aromatic smell of food.

Looking around the place, Lucy didn't like how eerie the yard looked. There was tall grass everywhere, and the trees had no leaves. The house was in bad shape, with its windows broken and the front door looking like it could come down at any moment.

"Whoever's staying here's not a good housekeeper," she said awkwardly.

The kids then walked to the door, afraid it could fall on them. Anna then stepped forward and tapped on the door.

KNOCK! KNOCK!

After knocking on the door, they waited for whoever lived in this poor old house. After a minute in the cold darkness, no one came to answer. Feeling more nervous, the kids decided to turn around and walk out of place, realizing that it may not be worth it.

Suddenly, they heard the door click. As they turned back, they saw the wooden door open, creaking as it slowly revealed the interior within. And there, behind the door...

There was no one...

The kids were more scared, seeing that the door, which was closed before, somehow opened without anyone doing it. They looked at each other, unsure of what to do next. Soon, the smell of the food pulled them in again, and they walked towards the entrance.

They stepped into the house and looked around the shabby hallway, with stairs going up toward the second floor. The kids kept viewing until the door behind them closed and slammed shut...

The kids jumped in panic, scared stiff. They shivered and shivered, afraid of who might live here. Could it be a ghost? Maybe that explained why the door opened and closed on its own. They were about to try and flee when suddenly, Noah let out a small yelp!

Everyone looked up, and they, too, saw a frightening sight. Up at the very top was an old woman, wrinkly and not so fit, staring somewhat angrily at the children. Her grumpy look made the kids mortified. She was holding a cane, tapping it roughly on her other palm.

She then pointed her sharp cane at the kids, revealing a pointy tip that looked like it could cut through metal! The group shivered again, afraid to see the cane's sharp tip pointing dangerously at them. When they looked at the old lady, she growled, "You four better come up here." Her low voice made it sound like a threat.

The children grew even more afraid as they saw the elderly lady walk into a room. They wanted to run, but she called out to them,

"Quick! Get up here!" Her shrieking voice made them all panic. With no other choice, the kids went up together. When they came to the room, the old lady looked away from them, stirring something in a black pot. The fire glowed so bright within the dark room, making it more ominous.

The kids walked in, waiting to be dealt the punishment for trespassing. The woman turned around, staring right into their eyes. The group was murmuring under their breath, feeling the doom coming. The old lady then grabbed her cane and walked toward them. The kids closed their eyes, waiting to be dealt with, and made victims of her wrath!

And then she asked, "Why are you wearing such silly costumes?!" She had *laughed*. The kids opened their eyes to see the old lady laugh! She finished chortling and looked at the kids again. This time, they saw that her face had changed. No more was she stern or angry. Now, she appeared to be bubbly and happy!

The children couldn't believe what they saw. The old lady who seemed so haunting was actually a kind old woman. She told them to sit down and relax. So, the children went to sit on a couch in the lounge area. The woman came by with four bowls of soup. The kids immediately recognized the smell of the soup as the delicious aroma they had found earlier.

Feeling so hungry, they drank up the soup, letting the taste flow in their mouths. The old lady chuckled in their faces before she asked them again.

"What are you all doing in my house?"

"We were just wondering what this smell was," Kevin explained.

"Well, enjoy yourselves!" the old lady offered. "People don't come to visit me because my house looks so haunted."

While they agreed, the kids chose not to say anything about it. About the costumes, they told her that it was Halloween, a time of costumes and treats.

"Treats, you say?" the old lady asked. "Come with me!" She gestured for them to follow her, leading them to a room at the back. They entered and saw a huge stack of chocolates and muffins stored on shelves. The kids were thrilled. Look at all the candy, they thought!

The woman then made them sit down and enjoy the delicious and sweet candies in the room. But the kids had to go home as the night had become dark. They thanked the old lady for giving them her treats and walked off.

As they were returning home, they laughed and joked about their miraculous visit to the old lady's house. However, when Anna looked at her wrist, she squealed, "Oh, no! My bracelet is gone!"

The group panicked. That was her favorite gold bracelet. Wanting to help Anna, the group decided to help her find it. The last time she remembered, Anna had her bracelet in the old lady's house. So, it was decided that they would go back to find it.

They returned to the old lady's house, opening the metal gate. But when they went through, they were horribly shocked to find that the house...was gone! The kids couldn't believe their eyes! The house that was there a few minutes ago had now disappeared into thin air. They were inside that house for an hour, eating chocolates and talking to a nice old lady!

Then Anna found her bracelet in the tall grass but was still shocked to find there was no house.

They looked everywhere until an old man walked by, shouting out to the kids. "Hey, you four!" he yelled. "What are you doing there?!"

The kids then told the man about the house that was now gone. They told him about the old lady who had given them sweets not long ago. The old man seemed to become very afraid when they finished talking. His face revealed his shock; he was mumbling as he looked down at the floor. When they asked why he was so scared, he told them everything.

As it turned out, the house was rumored to have been burned down in a fire. In that house lived a witch who was working on a spell to hide her dead husband. And just when things couldn't get worse, the witch might have *eaten* her husband!

Horrified by the man's tale, the kids realized why the house was empty, and no one had come at all. The old lady was a witch! Worse still, they began to fear that they had eaten chocolate made by a witch!

Suddenly, the kids felt something wrong in their stomachs. They began to feel very sick, holding their stomachs as they rumbled. Both afraid and in pain, the kids lay on the floor, falling victim to whatever they had eaten. They had become the victims of a witch!

Kevin was crying from the pain in his stomach, unable to stop it. Then, he tried to move his bandaged hand and rub his stomach, feeling the pain go away. After a while, it was all over, and Kevin could slowly move his hand away from his stomach.

Wait...! He could move his hand?! Kevin looked at his fingers and moved them. To his utter shock, the fingers did not hurt! Then, he removed the bandages and saw that his hand, previously bruised and broken, was completely fine!

After the other kids were free from the pain, they saw Kevin dancing around joyfully, seeing his arm was moving freely again! They were wondering how this could have happened! How could have Kevin's arm been healed after just a few hours?!

They realized something from their time in this place. Could it be that the chocolate they had eaten had helped heal Kevin's arm? Could it be that the old witch, who was believed to have eaten her husband, actually helped them after all?

The kids didn't know what to believe. Did the old lady want to kill or help them? Who's to say? But unknown to the kids, there was a presence from behind the wall watching them. The figure laughed mischievously as she turned away and flew into the night sky.

The little witch had played her tricks, and now, the kids could have their treats.

The Uninvited Guest

Collin was sitting in his room, working on his homework when he heard the sound of the telephone ringing.

RRRINGG!!! RRRIIINGGG!!! A phone call echoed through the house. The ringing made Collin jump up and run to the phone, only to see his father pick it up. As Collin watched his father talk on the phone, he saw disappointment on his face. After the call ended, Collin's father turned to him and said, "That was one of your uncles."

Collin's face drooped. His father always told him how "boring" their many relatives were.

"He said a friend of your grandpa is going to be in town and coming to visit," Collin's father added.

"Who is this friend, Dad?" Colin asked, hopeful that this friend of his grandfather was someone fun. Alas, his dad did not smile.

"I'm... not sure, son. I also don't know him well."

Collin knew his dad was not at all pleased about having this random person coming to visit their house. This was especially true since an uncle told him, someone he had not talked to in a long time. Whoever this person was, his dad didn't seem to like him all that much.

To get to know this stranger more, Collin asked his dad, "What does this guy do?" Collin saw his dad roll his eyes, then sigh.

"He said he is a paranormal investigator."

Collin's heart soared upon hearing the word "paranormal investigator." Someone experienced in finding ghosts! He couldn't be any more thrilled about meeting someone who could chase away evil spirits. After years of quietness and boredom, he could talk to a mysterious person for a change.

The next day, the phone rang again. Collin answered and heard an older man speaking in a friendly voice through the line. When Collin asked who it was, the man responded that he was the paranormal investigator and was about to arrive soon. Collin couldn't be any more excited.

"So, my boy, do you want me to get you anything? What do you like?" the man asked. Collin was becoming happier after being offered something by this paranormal investigator. What could he ask for from someone so mysterious? Some ghostly materials? A cool device to trap spirits?

Collin was about to answer the man about what he wanted. However, before he spoke, the man talked...only for his voice to disappear into static. Collin shook his phone, thinking he was losing reception. He went around the house for a good signal, hoping to reach back to the older man.

Collin went down to the basement in desperation, switching on the light. In the lit room, he listened out for the other person. However, as he put his ear close to the phone, he heard...

HUFF... HUFF...

Every second came the sound of heavy breathing, which Collin felt was somewhat strange. When he asked the man if he were still there, there came the sound of humming in a harmonious melody that somehow made Collin feel a little uncomfortable.

Thankfully, the man was still there, asking the question again. Calmed down, Collin asked if he could have a cat since his parents didn't allow him to have one. To that question, all Collin got in response was...silence. The call had ended. Collin was left to wonder what had happened, not uttering a word.

"Collin!" The boy was startled by his mother's stern call from upstairs. "You're not supposed to be there by yourself! Come up now!"

Collin was wondering why being in the basement was such a problem. Still, he knew better than to question his mother's authority. The basement was dark and creepy, after all. So, he left the basement, leaving him without an answer from the older man.

Later that week, another call came. Collin's parents were told that the guest was arriving at the airport, and they would have to go and fetch him. Because he had a project for school the next day, the boy could not go with them. Before they left, they told Collin to keep the doors closed until they came back. Though he didn't like being left alone again, Collin did not argue. He did what was told and locked up all the doors and windows, waiting for Mom and Dad to return with their guest.

Hours passed since his parents had left, and Collin had just finished doing his homework. He looked at his clock and saw with surprise that it was half past nine. After putting away his homework, he strolled down the steps and into the living room to watch TV until his parents returned.

As he watched cartoons, Collin could not hold in his excitement. The guest would arrive and shower him with fun and mystery any minute now! Alas, time went by and no one came home. Worried about his parents, Collin got up and went to the phone to call his dad. Then, just when he was about to ring his dad...

KNOCK!!! KNOCK!!!

The door was knocked hard, shocking the timid boy. Collin stared at the door as it remained silent. After that, another two knocks rapped at the door. Curious, Collin walked up to the door and looked through the eyehole. There outside the door, he found a man waiting with a smile.

He was slightly older than Collin's father, with wrinkles and greying hair. The boy was looking at a man who seemed polite and happy... but he was creeped out by this stranger. His mom told him not to answer to anyone, so he kept quiet.

However, his curiosity got the best of him, so he walked up to the door and looked through the eyehole again. There, he saw the man, still smiling, holding a bag in his hand. What could be in that bag, Collin wondered. So, he called out from behind the door and said,

"Who is it?" To this, the man replied, "It's me. Your guest, Mr. Phillip!" the man laughed with a welcoming chuckle.

Collin's heart sank with relief. He recognized the voice of the man from the call he had had. Excited that the guest had finally arrived, he quickly unlocked the door and opened it up, revealing a nice gentleman with the bag in hand.

With a shake of the hand and a laugh, Collin welcomed Mr. Phillip into the house. However, when he looked behind, he saw that his parents were not there? Didn't they say they would fetch Mr. Phillip from the airport? Where were they?

Then, Mr. Phillip called from behind, snapping him out of his thoughts.

"Is everything all right, boy?" he asked. Collin shook his head and asked,

"Where are my parents?" he asked.

"Oh! Your parents came to look for me? I'm sorry, boy," the old man laughed as he rubbed Collin's head, accelerating his awkwardness. "My plane arrived earlier than expected, so I decided to come here myself."

"I told your parents I'd be here," he added. "They should be back home soon."

Collin's body relaxed. Thank goodness, he thought. Then Mr. Phillip looked up the stairs and asked, "Where is the washroom?" Collin pointed to where it was: up the stairs and toward the left.

The man walked up without saying a word, slowly creeping his way to the washroom.

Once Mr. Phillip was inside the room, Collin went to the phone and called his parents. His mother answered the call. "Mom," Collin spoke. "Where are you?"

"I'm coming home now, sweetie," she said. "Make sure you get ready for Mr. Phillip."

At that moment, Collin's mind twisted with confusion.

"But Mom... Mr. Phillip... is here already. He called you, remember?"

"Wh-what?!" Collin heard his mother gasp. "What are you talking about?"

"He's here," Collin said, getting more nervous, "in the restroom." Before Collin could speak, his mother interrupted with a shaky voice...

"Collin! I need you to get out of the house! Right now!" she yelled with alarm. Collin was struck by fear and worry. Why was his mother screaming like he was in danger? Was Mr. Phillip not the friendly man his dad had told him about?

Then again... he remembered something else. Why did Mr. Phillip say he called his parents if they somehow didn't know he was there? Collin's heart grew even more pained, fear spreading across his body and mind. Suddenly, the dreadful news had come too late. He had let an absolute stranger into the house...

"I will call the cops, honey! Please run outside... NOW!"

With the urgent call over, the boy made a run for the door and out of the house. Suddenly, he heard a voice calling to him. It was "Mr. Phillip".

"Collin, can you come here?" Collin turned around with fright. He looked to expect the stranger upstairs only to find that he wasn't there. Freaking out, the boy looked around until he heard the man call again. "There's something I want to show you!"

But what terrified Collin more was that the man was not upstairs. Instead, the voice came from the deep, dark basement - the one place where he was told *not* to go into. He looked down the steps to see the dark room with nothing in sight.

Nothing... except for a dark silhouette. The shady figure walked like a phantom in the night, smiling eerily at Collin. The boy could hardly move or talk, frozen with fear. His heart beat faster than before, overcome by fright as the old man called out to him... with a gruesome voice!

"Come quick. I have a surprise for you."

Finally, Collin ran as fast as he could, dashing outside the door. As he ran, he saw two cars pull up. One was his family car and the other was the cops. Out of the family station wagon emerged

Collin's mom; she ran to give the boy an overbearing hug. Collin cried and cried, so wracked with fear over the wicked stranger's presence.

As his mother comforted him, he laid his eyes on his father behind them. He was accompanied by an older man who looked to be in his sixties. He seemed gentle and friendly, but Collin was still unsure.

"Relax, dear boy. I'm the real Mr. Phillip," he spoke with a voice gentler and calmer than the imposter in the house. Though slightly relieved, Collin was still shaking from what he saw. Then, two police officers ran into the house with a pair of handcuffs, ready to apprehend the man inside.

After an hour, as Collin's parents kept the boy close, the cops exited the building. With confused looks on their faces, they reported not to have not seen anyone. Collin was flabbergasted. He saw the man in the basement and heard his voice calling to him. How could he have escaped so quickly?

"Did you check the basement?" Collin asked.

"Yes," one of the cops replied. "But we found nothing."

"Nothing except for this bag," the other cop said, holding a black bag in his hand. Collin immediately recognized it as the bag the fake Mr. Phillip had been holding. The cop placed the bag down and opened it up.

As soon as the zip opened, everyone was in pure shock! Inside the bag to their disgust and horror was a dead cat, barely rotting away. Close to vomiting, Collin vaguely remembered telling Mr. Phillip that he wanted a cat for a pet.

In the end, no one seemed to know who or what that man was. Why did he come to the house for Collin? Knowing he had brought a dead cat into the house, what vile things could he have done?

With the horrifying ordeal over, Collin and his family returned to the house with Mr. Phillip, who offered to keep watch. After all, the imposter's arrival seemed too shady to be a criminal act. As they had entered the house, Mr. Phillip froze, overcome by dread. Collin's dad asked him what was wrong. The only thing he was given was a frightened stare.

Mr. Phillip shivered as he sat down in the living room. With shocked looks, the family was told what he had sensed. Their response was pure terror.

"Your house....it's haunted. I sense it. An evil spirit has visited this place."

Collin gasped in horror while his mom hugged him tightly, thinking of the worst outcome that could have happened. At last, the family decided to move out of their haunted house, hoping to find a better, more peaceful place to live. As for Mr. Phillip, he remained in town to investigate the spirit who had donned his identity.

Whatever happened next, Collin was sure to keep this terrifying memory, for he never knew if the man who called for him... would ever return...

A Chilly Night

It was the busiest time of the year as Christmas was around the corner. The holiday season is supposed to be a joyful time - a time to go home and be free from work. Derek was one of the unlucky ones. He had to work extra hours in the coffee shop and left to make drinks for others who *could* celebrate the holidays. The barista sighed as he cleaned a smudged cup, wanting to go home and relax.

Derek looked to the door to see a customer leave the store. He checked the cash register and saw that he had earned a good profit that day. As he looked outside the shop's tinted window, Derek wondered about the shop's odd location. His boss thought it was a good idea to build a shop in the middle of nowhere as there were no other shops around, where drivers could park between trips to rest and have a drink.

Only one customer was left, who was sipping his last drop of Americano. Once he left the shop, Derek looked at the clock and saw that it was almost ten o'clock, which was when his shift ended. Packing up for the night, he went to close the shop and head home. When he looked out the door, he saw snow fluttering down all over the place, covering the road with a blanket of white.

Feeling so cold, he went back to the staff room to get his coat and get warm for the trip home. Grabbing his bag, he was about to walk out of the room. Suddenly, Derek heard a faint wailing sound coming from outside. He could have sworn that he was the only person left in the building. But he supposed that someone had come right before he could close up.

Derek opened the door and looked out to find a woman walking about frantically, looking around like a lost lamb. He could see her distraught back as she looked around one of the tables. Sighing, Derek walked towards her, reaching his hand out to get her attention. He cleared his throat before calling to the woman and touching her shoulder to turn her around.

As the woman faced him, Derek let out a horrified gasp. The woman's face covered in nothing...but blood! Dried blood was splattered on her forehead, reaching all the way down her neck and dress. Upon seeing this gruesome sight, Derek backed away. But when he stepped back, the woman ran toward him, frightening Derek even more. Her hands grabbed him so hard that it was almost like she was about to tackle him. Her palms felt ice cold on his shoulders, while her face was pale and blue as ice. She then spoke in a voice that was quiet yet eerie at the same time.

"Please... I need help..." she croaked. "There was an accident... My daughter... She's in the car. She's stuck...."

Derek's heart sank, and his horror intensified over the injured woman's situation. With urgency, he grabbed the phone to call the police for help. However, as he dialed the number, he began to wonder why hadn't she called the cops to come and rescue her daughter? She may have been injured, but she seemed capable of moving around and grabbing him. Also, why didn't she stay behind to watch over her daughter at a time when she needed her the most?

However, one look at the snow falling outside and Derek scolded himself for being inconsiderate. As the phone was ringing for the cops, he made the frantic woman sit on a chair, leaving her shaking wildly with fear. Soon, the cops responded, and an ambulance was on the way. All the while, the woman murmured under her breath, worried about her daughter. Derek offered her a cup of hot coffee, but she quickly refused.

Then, the woman asked Derek to find out if her daughter was okay, pleading for him to stay by her side until the cops arrived. Confused, he wondered why she couldn't do it herself. However, he agreed to go, telling her to stay at the store and wait out the snow. Someone had to stay by the little girl's side until help came.

Driving all the way to the accident site, Derek soon saw what had been told to him. To his horror, he saw a dented 1967 Chevy tipped upside down with smoke coming out of the engine. He got out of his car, eyes entirely focused on the destroyed vehicle before him. Thankfully, two police vehicles and an ambulance were at the scene. Two cops were standing in front of the site, arms crossed. The barista approached them, telling them that he was the one who had called.

The cops then told Derek that two people were inside the vehicle: a child and an elderly person. Wait... Derek thought. *Two* people? Why didn't the woman mention the elder person? Moreover, looking at where his store was, he wondered how she could escape the accident and walk an hour-long journey with her injuries.

Talking to the cops again, Derek said the woman was waiting for her daughter to be rescued at his store. The cops stayed silent for a while until one of them spoke, "The child is alive, sir," making Derek feel relieved. But what the cop said next, he was not prepared to hear... "But the driver is dead."

Hearing the news, Derek's heart shattered. Someone had died in the accident. Feeling sorry, he did not know how to give this news to the woman. Was it her husband, the girl's father? He hoped that she could handle the loss...

As Derek waited, he saw the cops finally save the little girl, putting her on a stretcher. The girl was covered in cuts on her cheeks and hands, with some bruises as well. He hoped she would be okay as she was placed in the ambulance.

Then Derek saw the cops trying to pull out the dead body in the driver's seat. They were having problems extracting it the damaged front. He overheard them describing how brutal the crash's impact was, saying the woman's head was almost smashed.

The *woman*? Okay, so it wasn't a man. But what saddened Derek even more was that she was seen holding the hand of the child as if she didn't want anything to happen to her.

Finally, after what felt like ten minutes, Derek saw the cops successfully removing the body out of the car. As the snow fell even harder, the barista's eyes shrank. His heart suddenly stopped as his whole body froze from absolute shock. Right in front of him, dead on the floor, the woman had the same bloodied forehead, with blood trailing down her neck. The body of the woman he saw terrified him. Not just because of how damaged it was, but what the woman looked like.

The woman who died was the woman he met in the store! Derek was horrified beyond belief. Not long ago, that same woman was alive in his shop, clearly out of the wrecked car. As he looked on, he saw the same injuries, her blue lips, and pale hands. He was so terrified that he was about to vomit.

Before he could fall to the floor, a cop came up to him and asked about the survivor said to be waiting at his shop. Derek did not say a word. He had no idea what to tell the officer. How could he? That "survivor" was now apparently dead.

It was like... he had seen a ghost.

With nowhere to go, Derek muttered the truth in a shaky voice. After hearing his story, the cop just gave him a sympathetic look and patted his shoulder, telling him that he was probably traumatized by the whole ordeal. Frankly, Derek didn't know what to say or do anymore. Thanking the cop, he took to his car and left the scene, unprepared for what he would find.

The woman was gone when he returned to the shop, much to his added horror. When he stepped inside, he still felt the sheer chill of her grasp on him, as if she were there. Running to the office room to check the CCTV, he was even more bewildered to find himself standing there...with no one else in sight. He was standing there like a madman, shaking all by himself. He even saw himself pull the chair out, where no one would sit.

At that point, Derek was about to sit down, ready to consider himself insane. But as he thought about it, the shop's doorbell had not chimed to indicate her entry. If nothing else, Derek realized that, perhaps, the woman *did* come to him. He didn't *feel* that he had seen a ghost Derek *did* see a ghost... and she had come to seek help for her daughter.

Mirror, Mirror on the Wall

One summer ago, a woman named Katy moved to a new house with her two kids, Alex and Emily. She was a single mother left to raise her children on her own. After living out of the city for so long, the family decided to relocate.

During her move, Katy met the old realtor who offered her the house, hoping to make the final payment. The woman told her that the previous owner was generous enough to leave all the furniture behind, saying they already had what they needed. But she left a rather stern warning never to remove the covers off the mirrors in the house. If they were removed, she warned, bad things could happen.

Katy was suspicious, but she chose to heed the "warning". After all was said and done, the family finally settled into their new home. While cleaning up, Katy saw the covered mirrors. She couldn't see the glass underneath the cloth, but she did catch a glimpse of the edges, which were beautifully carved.

Although she was still confused about the warning, she decided to go along with it, assuming that the mirrors were broken. And you know what they say: broken mirrors mean seven years of bad luck...

To convince Alex and Emily not to remove the covers, Katy lied, telling them that the mirrors were indeed broken and she didn't want them to get injured.

One night, sometime after the move was complete, Katy was peacefully asleep, resting after a day's worth of chores. But as she was deep in dreams, she was rudely awakened by the sound of a door opening. Getting up, she went to investigate, finding that the bathroom door was open.

Katy peeped into the room to find out what was happening. There she found Alex standing in front of the sink... looking in the mirror. As she looked in the mirror, she was shocked to find that the cover had been removed! She ran into the room, taking Alex by the arm. She asked him what he was doing in the middle of the night. The boy told her that he was about to go to the kitchen for a drink of water...

But then he told her that something called him. Alex said it was a low whisper, causing him to follow the sound, which led him to the mirror. Alex said the mirror had already lost its cover when he got there.

Confused again, Katy thought Alex was probably sleepwalking, so she took him back to his room and tucked him into bed. Soon after, she, too, returned to her bed, forgetting about the mirror.

The following day, Katy went to the bathroom, realizing that she had forgotten to close the cover on the mirror. However, this time, she got to see the mirror and found that it wasn't broken. Perhaps, the warning was false, after all?

When Emily asked if they could remove the covers of all the mirrors. Katy agreed; soon enough, all the sheets were removed. Not a single mirror was broken. In fact, they looked stunning with their antique-like designs. Katy wondered what the big fuss was about with the previous owner.

That night, Katy went to the bathroom again to have a shower. She stood in front of the beautiful mirror, wanting to check her face. She worked in the fashion industry, and her work demanded that she maintain her appearance. So, she washed her face, soaking it in water. As she moved her head up and opened her eyes, she saw her reflection in the mirror... and gasped.

There she saw that her entire face was gone! Staring at this empty face, she shook her head and washed it again. When she looked back, her reflection was there. She stared blankly at the mirror for a while, bewildered by what she had seen. She thought maybe she was working too hard and the stress was getting to her. So, she finished cleaning up and went to bed.

As she switched off the lights, Katy left the room unaware that the mirror summoned a reflection of herself...with an evil grin.

The next morning, Katy was in her room, getting dressed. She was getting ready to drop her kids off at school before heading to work. She was looking at her bedroom mirror while putting on her makeup. As she applied her lipstick, she saw Alex at the door. He was not wearing his pants, as he had been waiting for his mother to help him with his belt. As Katy was too focused on her makeup, she did not turn to face her son, only using his reflection to speak to him.

She told Alex to get ready or they would be late. The boy just left without putting on his pants. After that, Katy finished getting ready and left the room to help Alex. When she went downstairs, she saw Alex chatting with Emily at the table. There, she saw that he had managed to put on his pants after all!

Katy came down to compliment Alex for putting on his belt all by himself. However, when Alex turned to her, he said he was already prepared to leave about half an hour ago. Katy thought he was bluffing, but Emily assured her that he was telling the truth. This surprised Katy, so she asked if Alex had been in her room a while ago.

To her utter confusion, Alex said he didn't go there at all...

Katy was now feeling creeped out. First, she had seen that weird reflection last night. Now, she saw Alex's reflection in the bedroom mirror. Was she really that stressed out? Did she need to take the day off? She had no idea...

Regardless, Katy brushed it off and drove her kids to school. Alex quickly ran out of the car and into the building upon arrival. However, little Emily did not. Katy asked if she was okay, worried that something had happened. Emily shook her head, saying that something wasn't wrong at school.

To Katy's fright, Emily said something was wrong... with the house. She then told her mother that last night, she wanted to go to the bathroom. Then as she entered the room, she saw her reflection in the mirror.

Instead of following her every move, she said that her reflection smiled at her. The reflection called to her, asking her to come closer. When she came close, the reflection told her to touch the mirror.

"Did you touch it?" Katy asked with a surprised look. She can't be going mad, but something was happening in their house.

"No. I was scared, Mommy. So, I ran to the bathroom."

Afterward, Emily said that she had returned to her room after running out, only to find that her reflection was back to normal. Finishing her story, Emily sobbed with fright. Katy gave her daughter a warm hug, promising she would sleep with the kids that night.

After dropping off her kids at school, Katy decided to return home for the things she had forgotten to take. When she had returned home, she went to her room and picked up the items. As soon as she was ready to leave, she heard laughter...

Following the laughter, she came across her bedroom mirror. When she looked at it, she was horrified to see what was there. She could see reflections of her own children in the mirror! They looked at her with happy smiles on their faces, cheering,

"Mommy is back! Come here, Mommy! We missed you!"

Katy was frozen with fear, stepping back ever so slowly. As the kids egged her on, she turned around and ran out of the house, fear taking over her entire body. Now, things were really getting out of hand...

As she ran out of the house, Katy suddenly bumped into an old lad she recognized as her next-door neighbor. She asked if Katy was okay before inviting her into her house. The mother of two looked back at her house, fearing she was losing it. So, she accepted the offer and walked with the old lady.

In the lady's house, Katy told her everything that had happened. To her absolute horror, the old lady confirmed that the mirrors were indeed cursed! Worse still, she had unleashed the dreaded curse upon her house by opening up the covers.

The old lady told Katy how the mirrors became cursed. As it turned out, a man performed an exorcism that trapped evil souls in the mirrors as requested by his clients. One day, the man trapped one soul, which turned out to be the spirit of his dead wife. Overcome with grief, the man conjured a terrible spell that killed him. It was said that the wife's spirit killed him, and that anyone who tried to remove the mirrors would meet a fate worse than death.

Thus, it was decided to cover up the mirrors so the spirits could never escape. But a priest warned that if the mirrors were touched, the person would be swapped with their reflections, trapping the real person into the mirror for all eternity!

Frightened by this story, Katy was worried about her kids. After leaving the neighbor's house, she began to plan to move out of the house. That night, she covered up all the mirrors again, even though the curse had been unleashed.

Emily suddenly came down with a fever, so Katy had to leave her kids alone and go get some medicine. Upon returning, she opened the door...only to find that the house was pitch black. Every corner was dark with no shadows or light.

AAAAAHHHH!!!

Running into the house, Katy saw Emily curled up in bed, covered in a sheet. She went to free Emily and hugged her tightly as the girl sobbed. But when she looked for Alex, she was terrified to find him missing!

When she looked around the house, she found that all the mirrors were uncovered again, overwhelming her with absolute fear. Katy asked Emily what had happened. The girl told her that after she left, the lights had suddenly gone out. Alex volunteered to find some candles, and that was the last time she had seen him.

When Emily entered her room, the cover of her bedroom mirror suddenly threw itself down, revealing her evil reflection again. She screamed for Alex, but the boy was nowhere to be found.

Horrified, Katy knew that Alex was in danger. She grabbed Emily in her arms and took her out of the house. Putting her in the car, Katy ran back inside to find Alex. She couldn't find the boy everywhere she looked, now fearing the worst.

Suddenly, Katy heard a faint sound coming from the storage room.

"Mommy..." Katy's heart soared, recognizing the voice to be none other than Alex. She ran to the room and opened the door. There, to her utter relief, she found her son shaking in the corner in terrible fear. The room was full of mirrors stored by Katy because there were too many in the house. She quickly hugged Alex and took him out of the room.

Before leaving the room, she heard Alex's reflection in the mirror. When she turned around, she saw the image of her son crying. He smashed the mirror, shouting to her, "Mommy! Don't leave me!"

Fearing for their lives, Katy ran out of the room and out of the house. Back in her car, she started the engine and drove off. To take care of Alex, Emily hugged the boy. She turned to her mother and asked where they would go. Katy said they would go to a hotel until they could sort things out. She then asked if Alex was okay, only to find that he was silently humming. She thought he was trying to make himself feel better by singing his favorite song. Thus, she turned back to the road and drove on.

Alex hummed, looked out the window, and was staring into the night sky as Emily kept him close. As he looked on, he ducked his head... and grinned.

Sitting there, smirking coldly at the family, little Alex kept on humming. Unbeknownst to Katy, the boy sitting in the car wasn't her Alex at all. The little boy was trapped in the mirror back at the house while the kid sitting with them was a devil in disguise.

THANK YOU for purchasing this book and making it all the way to the end.

Before you go, I wanted to ask for a small favor. If you liked this book, would you mind taking a minute to post your review on Amazon (or at least mark the rating)?

Posting a review is the best and easiest way to support the work of independent authors like me.

Your feedback will help me to keep writing the kind of books that you want. It would mean a lot to me to hear from you.

To leave a quick review go to link:

amazon.com/dp/B0BQ9N76RP

Or scan QR code with your camera:

Thanks again, and I really look forward to reading your feedback!

DISCOVER OUR BEST BOOKS

Go to link:

amazon.com/stores/author/B0BN6R1P1X

Or scan QR code with your camera:

Made in the USA
Las Vegas, NV
27 November 2023

81685756R00069